Hey Diddle Diddle

Hey diddle diddle,

The cat and the fiddle,

The cow jumped over the moon.

The little dog laughed to see such sport,

And the dish ran away with the spoon.

adapted by Carrie Smith
illustrated by Bill Greenhead

Look at the cat.

Look at the cat play.

Look at the fiddle.

Look at the fiddle play.

Look at the cow.

Look at the cow jump.

Look at the moon.

Look at the moon smile.

Look at the dog.

Look at the dog laugh.

Look at the spoon.

Look at the dish.

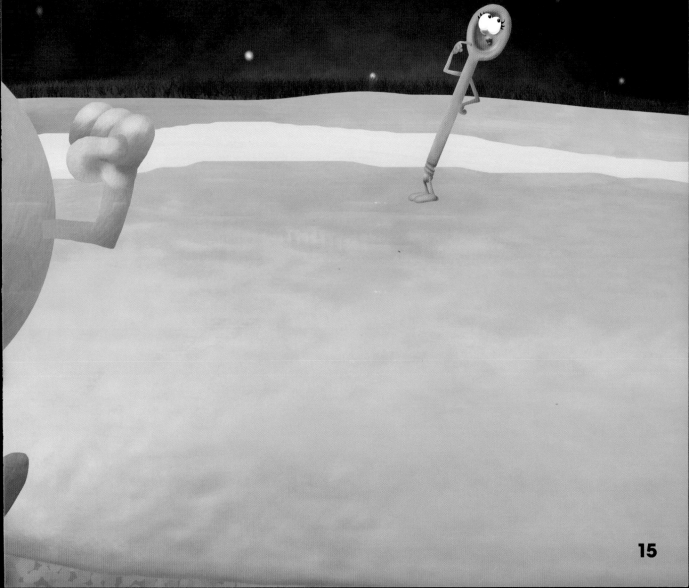

Look at them run.